Dedication

This book is dedicated to my beautiful daughter, Erin Olivia.
You are my biggest achievement in life,
Filling my life with love, laughter, and hope.
You are the sunshine on my rainy days.
My heart will be forever filled with love because of you.

About the Author

Leanne Brown, the author of Daniel's Dreams: Monster Mountain, lives is Greater Manchester, England with her partner Steve and her young daughter, Erin.

Leanne is a qualified secondary English teacher, who has specialised in special educational needs, and is now focusing on writing children's books based on mental health issues that arise in children. Mental health is something that Leanne is passionate about and hopes her books will help young children everywhere.

When not writing, Leanne likes to spend time with her family. She loves to read, colour, watch a good series or film, go swimming, enjoy a meal out and spending quality time with her daughter and partner.

Published in association with Bear With Us Productions

WRITTEN BY
LEANNE BROWN

ILLUSTRATED BY
YOGESH MAHAJAN

Chapter 1
Daniel and Darcie

Daniel sat with his family to have their tea. This was something they did every night; they would talk about their days and what they had done. Mum and Dad insisted on it. "Time at the table to talk and be together is important," they would say. Daniel liked it. He loved being with his family. But this evening was different. Daniel shifted restlessly in his chair as he struggled to sit still. There was something on his mind. Something that was unsettling him, and he couldn't focus properly on his meal. He pushed his food around his plate and Mum interrupted his thoughts.

"So, what have we done today?" Mum asked, whilst she passed the broccoli.

Dad talked about how he had meetings, taken phone calls and all the usual boring stuff parents seem to do when they go to work.

"Well, Amelia and I had a falling out today and Miss Rodgers had to speak to us," announced Darcie, Daniel's younger sister.

"Oh dear. Now what was that all about?" Dad asked with a roll of his eyes.

Daniel listened as Darcie went on and on about how her and Amelia had wanted to use the special paint brush and only one of them could get to use it. Amelia won and this upset Darcie. Really upset her. As Darcie

continued with her story, Daniel began to feel strange. He was there at the table and he could hear Darcie talking, but he didn't feel like he was processing what she had said. He heard bits of the story but then his mind would wander.

"Daniel, Daniel. Daniel, are you OK?" Mum's words reached him through the fog in his mind.

"Oh yeah, sorry, Mum. What were you asking?" Daniel asked embarrassed.

I said, "How was your day at school?"

"It was fine," Daniel replied in a low tone.

"Is everything OK, Daniel? It's just you're incredibly quiet and you've hardly eaten anything," Mum asked with a loving touch of his arms.

"I just don't feel very hungry and I've got those bug things in my belly again." Daniel was sad and lowered his head.

"You mean butterflies?" Dad asked with a smile.

"Yeah, butterflies," Daniel whispered.

"Daniel, everything is going to be OK. It's OK to be nervous. It's natural," Mum reassured him.

"It sure is! You'll be amazing!" Darcie added with excitement and a mouth full of food.

"Remember, butterflies in your belly aren't always a bad thing. They can be signs of excitement too," Dad told him.

Their words helped to settle Daniel's thoughts for a little while, but they didn't take away the fact that something unpleasant was looming.

After tea, Daniel helped clear the plates and went to get ready for his bath. Typically, the bathroom was covered with water; it was everywhere; in places you wouldn't even know water could reach! This was a clear sign that Darcie had been in the bath first and had very much enjoyed it too – it looked like a waterfall had burst everywhere! Daniel's parents often compared Darcie's bath time to bathing a dolphin.

Once bathed, Daniel heard his mum shout that their hot chocolates were ready. He still felt butterflies in his stomach. He wanted to believe everything would be OK, he wished he could believe in himself. Darcie flew out of her bedroom, grabbed Daniel's arm, and dragged him down the stairs. He would have to solve his worries later.

As night closed in slowly, the stars twinkled brightly in the dark sky. The icy cold air wrapped itself around Daniel and his sister as they finished off their warming hot chocolates.

"Straight up to bed after those hot chocolates," Mum said firmly. "You have an important day tomorrow."

"Aww, but, Mum!" Darcie complained.

"No complaining, Darcie!" Mum exclaimed.

"I'll be right up," said Daniel eagerly.

Darcie always tried to argue for more time before she had to go to sleep. She was a fiery little girl, with a soft spot for her brother. Daniel often thought she got away with most things because she had a cute smile; but he knew she was strong and independent too.

Bedtime was Daniel's favourite time of the day; he knew he would meet new people, go on great adventures, and experience different feelings. Every night he visited somewhere new, someone new. He always did!

Daniel ran up the stairs in record speed. He brushed his teeth, shouted goodnight, and jumped into bed; his worries forgotten.

Daniel took some deep, calming breaths as he did every night to help him fall asleep. He drifted off to sleep knowing that his journey for the night was just about to begin, he didn't know where he would end up or who he would meet, but he did know it would be fun.

Chapter 2
Daniel and Darcie

Daniel slowly opened his eyes, a piercing light shone into them and startled him, he pulled the duvet up to his chin. As he peered over his soft duvet cover, he spotted someone, something! He was unsure at what was staring back at him and that made him feel uneasy. This 'thing' was like nothing he had seen before. He was excited, but nervous. The butterflies in his belly were back. He remembered Mum saying that butterflies could be a good feeling too. The piercing light dimmed a little and he felt himself relax, this was the sign he was waiting for, his journey had begun; he was in his dreams and his adventure was about unfold.

"Hey! Hey, come on. Wake up!" 'the thing' shouted.

Daniel tried to focus his eyes so he could make out what exactly 'the thing' was that was standing at the side of his bed.

"Who... who are you?" Daniel asked curiously.

"Come on, we've got adventures to go on. I've got to get back quickly tonight. Come on, come on!" 'The thing' shook him with excitement.

Daniel sat up, rubbed his eyes and looked around. This was his bedroom, but 'the thing' looking back at him was not something he normally saw in his bedroom. He needed a moment to compose himself and remember he was in his dreams.

In front of him stood a tall, squidgy looking... not a thing... a monster! The monster was corn yellow, with an egg-shaped body that had two spindly long eyes sticking out the top of his head. A long, ruby red tongue slipped in and out of his mouth. Strangely, he wore a pair of denim blue jeans that looked like they belonged on a human not a monster, but no t-shirt.

"You're, you're a MONSTER!" Daniel screamed, trembling as he sat up.

"I sure am," the monster said in an overly excited tone. "Pleased to meet you. I'm Dex." He offered out his hand, which was long and thin, with jelly dripping from it. Dex did not seem concerned that Daniel was scared of him.

"Ye... ye... yeah nice to meet you," said Daniel sheepishly.

"No need to be afraid... not all monsters are scary, you know," Dex said in a serious tone with his hands on his hips. "In fact, my friends and I can be quite good fun and some of us are super cool, just like me." Dex was swinging his body around as if to show off exactly how cool he was.

"You should never judge someone just because of how they look. That's what we all say to one another anyway," Dex spoke with confidence.

Daniel looked down and mumbled, "I'm sorry if I upset you. I just wasn't expecting to see... you know... monsters. Who is 'we'?" Daniel looked around. "Are there more monsters here?"

"Oh, you know, me and my other monster friends, back in the village. There's a whole lot of us. All different and unique. If you think I look odd, wait until you meet the others!" Dex said proudly.

"So, there's more of you?" Daniel wondered what the other monsters would look like. "I'd love to meet them

too. My name's Daniel by the way!"

"Nice to meet you, Daniel. Do you want to come and meet my friends? I'm sure they would love to meet you too! But we have got to get going. I have to be back in time tonight." Dex gave a funny giggle.

"What's so funny?" Daniel asked confused, looking himself up and down.

"You look funny; a little different to us," Dex said with a smile.

"I thought we didn't judge what people looked like," Daniel reminded him.

"You're right, sorry. We've got to go. Can't be late!" Dex said eagerly.

"Absolutely!" said Daniel with great excitement. He jumped to his feet and brushed himself off. "Let's go!" he shouted as he stood with Dex.

So far this looked like it would be a special adventure. Daniel loved how his dreams took him to new places and he got to meet different people, beings and things. Every night was something new and this was the start of tonight's journey.

"Firstly, we have to get there. Now, let me try and remember the rhyme to get us there." Dex scratched his chin.

"A rhyme?" questioned Daniel.

"Yeah, we have to say a rhyme to get us on our way. Everyone is waiting so let's get going. Shelley is coming tonight and it's really important we are all there," Dex said with great excitement.

"Shelley?" questioned Daniel. "And coming where?"

"Yeah, I'll explain when we get there," Dex said hurriedly.

"Take a breath and close your eyes,
To visit places filled with butterflies.
Magical places old and new,
Meet unique monsters and take in the view.

At Monster Mountain we will stop,
Run, jump, play and maybe hop.
A land of unique, independence and hope,
Where we can be ourselves and learn to cope."

Dex said this slowly and with care. Trying not to mess up the words. He took Daniel's hand and they closed their eyes.

A tingle fizzled up Daniel's body; from his head to his toes. Dex still had hold of his hand - it was slimy and squidgy.

"Open your eyes. We're here!" Dex whispered to Daniel.

Daniel's eyes remained closed; he was a little nervous, unsure of what he would see. His hands felt sweaty.

"It's OK, Daniel, you're safe here. There is nothing to worry about." Daniel felt Dex squeeze his hand for reassurance. As he squeezed his hand, the slime squidged between their hands and made a funny noise. Both Daniel and Dex laughed.

"Sounds like Arlo's bum when he eats too many beans!" Dex laughed.

Although he loved the adventures he went on in his dreams, Daniel was a shy and timid child. There were times, especially at school, when he would feel worried and often needed to be encouraged by others.

"Take a deep breath and open your eyes. I'm right next to you," Dex said calmly.

Daniel took a deep breath and calmed his nerves. He didn't know what to expect or where he would be when he opened his eyes. In fact, he didn't even know who would be staring back at him either. Daniel slowly opened his eyes, what he saw before him was something truly magical, something he had never seen before. He was finally at the destination of tonight's dream.

Chapter 3
Monster Mountain

"This place, it's... it's... it's just magical!" Daniel exclaimed, spinning around and taking in the sights his eyes were drinking in.

It was beautiful. Daniel was awestruck. It was like nothing he had seen before. He had been on many adventures in his dreams, but this place was different, it was unique. It was truly special.

Daniel had opened his eyes to discover he was on the top of a steep hill. The grass was emerald green and luscious. To each side of him, Daniel could see the hills rolling for what seemed like miles and miles.

"What is this place? *Where* is this place?" Daniel asked in amazement.

"This is Monster Mountain. This is home." There was pride in Dex's voice.

"I think it's beautiful. I don't think there's anything monstrous about it!" Daniel smiled.

"That's because everyone thinks monsters are mean, but we aren't. We are different that's all," Dex admitted shyly.

Daniel spotted something twinkling out of the corner of his eye. It glistened like snow in the wintertime and he was desperate to know what it was. Before he could ask, Dex was encouraging him to come and meet his other monster friends.

"Let's go!" Dex said.
Dex pointed down the hill, which immediately caught Daniel's attention. At the bottom of the hill, he could see a village. Daniel was going to meet Dex's friends and see where they all lived. Daniel had butterflies in his stomach again. He knew he needed to deal with them, but he was too excited and tried to push them to one side.

Daniel and Dex walked down the hill in the direction of the houses. As they grew closer to the village, they came across a sign that said, 'Welcome to Monster Mountain the village of uniqueness and difference." The sign was dripping with slime, but Daniel didn't think this unusual after seeing Dex's hands.

"Why is it called Monster Mountain?" asked Daniel inquisitively.

"Because sometimes what we all face in life is a mountain to be climbed. But with the right encouragement, we can get over it. The view from the top of a mountain is like looking forward into the future, and is definitely worth the climb," Dex explained.

Daniel twirled his body round to take in the beauty he saw before him. As he stopped, he spotted the twinkle that caught his eye earlier; in front of him was a large clock tower. It was a very special clock tower. Daniel saw the face of the clock glistening in diamonds. Beautiful, pure, sparkling diamonds. It was magnificent! In the sunlight it shone as far as Daniel could see. He smiled as he noticed the numbers on the clock were all upside down and backwards. He giggled and wondered how they could ever be on time for anything when the clock was always wrong. Monster Mountain was so beautiful, calm even. Daniel realised that he felt relaxed here, that he hadn't even thought about the dreaded task tomorrow, his worries had faded somehow.

5

Hello

B

G

K

As the two of them reached the houses, Daniel could see that this was not like any other town he had seen or been to before, this was uniquely different, truly odd, but oh so wonderful! The houses were different colours; blue, green, red, yellow, orange and everything else in between. There were round houses, square houses, triangular houses, every shape, and size. They appeared to have their own personalities. Daniel liked this. He noticed that the letterboxes curled up and smiled at him as he walked through the village. He even saw the windows wink at him! Some houses said 'hello' and some played beautiful music through their chimneys. Daniel wondered what the monsters must look like if these were the houses, they lived in.

Central to the village was a grassland where Daniel could see a circular seating area and a roaring campfire. Around the seating was an array of colours, textures, sizes; these were Dex's monster friends; they had to be. Daniel's hands began to tremble, and his stomach felt fluttery, but he told himself this was normal when you meet someone new. He had experienced feelings like this before. He thought back to the day he met Ryan, his best friend, on the first day of school. He felt so nervous his belly was filled with butterflies and his hands were sweaty. That wasn't too bad after all, so, he took a deep breath, smiled and walked towards the campfire.

"Hey everyone, this is Daniel. I found him sleeping in his bedroom. Actually, he was making some strange noises," said Dex, scratching his head in thought.

Heads turned, some all the way around, and every single eye was looking at Daniel – and there were a lot of eyes; Daniel had never seen so many. Some of Dex's friends had more than two eyes, some he wouldn't even like to count. He could feel every eye analysing him. Daniel hoped they weren't eying him up for lunch.

"Hi everyone," Daniel said apprehensively.

There were groans, grunts, rumbles, mumbles, heys and hellos from all around. Some of the monsters were waving, some laughing, some were lowering their heads and continuing with their conversations. Daniel could hear whispers about Shelley coming tonight. He thought back to when Dex had mentioned that he needed to be back for Shelley. He wondered who Shelley was and why tonight was so important.

"Dex?" Daniel asked. "Who is Shelley?"

"Shelley is one of our monster friends here in Monster Mountain. Sadly, she hasn't made it to a meeting yet. She gets worried and it upsets her. She really struggles to talk in front of all of us. But we have been trying for a while to help her and to get her here tonight. We want to help her and hopefully we have," Dex explained.

"I understand what that feeling is like," Daniel replied. "But what is tonight? What is it she will be coming to?"

But the sight of a monster bouncing up and down, talking fast and waving at him furiously, interrupted Daniel's questions. He smiled shyly and waved back.

"That's Octo!" Dex told him.

"Is he always this excited?"

"He sure is! Sometimes he can't sit still. We just embrace him; he talks a lot too," Dex said and Daniel loved the way he spoke about him with such acceptance.

Daniel could hear giggling as he watched two younger monsters chasing each other and laughing. This reminded him of when he and Darcie played hide-and-seek and the fun they had together. Darcie would love it here. A monster near the campfire was busy tidying away leaves that had blown aimlessly near the campfire. She was picking each one up and straightening the benches around the fire and muttering to herself. Daniel couldn't quite hear what she was saying as she picked up leaf after leaf.

"Who is that?" Daniel asked Dex.

"That's Bessie. She likes things tidy and just-so," Dex lowered his voice.

In the far-right corner, Daniel could hear a large foghorn noise coming from a monster blowing her nose. He looked and spotted a tear rolling down her face and she gently wiped it away with one of her many tentacles. The noise was so loud it made some of the monsters chuckle. He heard one of them make a comment about, "smelling wind" but Daniel knew the noise was nose blowing and not wind. Darcie was a wind breaker; this made Daniel smile as he thought about his sister.

"That's Shadow." Dex pointed to the monster who was sobbing.

Daniel and Dex were disturbed by a loud noise. Daniel couldn't ask Dex why Shadow was crying, but he would try to find out when he could, he liked to help people especially if they were upset.

BANG! BANG! BANG!

Daniel jumped at the loud noise coming from the left side of the campfire. A round monster, who was a fiery red colour and had misshapen blobs around his body, was whacking a wooden plank against the floor! From a distance, Daniel was convinced there was steam coming out of his ears, but he couldn't be certain. It reminded him of when Darcie got angry with her dolls for not drinking all the pretend tea she had made them.

The monster shouted, "Why me, why is it always me? What is wrong with this place? Why can't it just fit into the space I spent all day creating for it? Stupid plank of wood. Well, that will teach you!"

The plank broke in two and the monster seemed

satisfied, but his face was redder than before, and he seemed to be sweating.

"That's Wallop," whispered Dex.

Daniel thought it best not to introduce himself to the Wallop just yet rather opting to give him some time to calm down. He knew that having some time to calm down always worked when he felt angry. Although he couldn't ever remember breaking things.

"Going to have to do some planking later!" shouted a monster called Charm to Dex.

"We plank in PE!" Daniel said, feeling proud about making links between his world and the monster world.

"It's not an exercise, silly, he means planks to replace the one Wallop's just broken," Dex said with a smile. "Take a seat, it's about to begin!"

Chapter 4
The Campfire

"Find a seat, Daniel, anywhere you can," Dex said loudly.

The excitement could be felt and heard all around the campfire. There were still whispers about Shelley coming and how wonderful it will be for her to overcome her fear, how it would be an achievement for her. Even though he had not met her yet, Daniel felt excited for Shelley. He too wanted her to succeed and overcome her fear. He was glad to be there to witness a big moment for her.

Daniel was about to sit down when he heard, "Not that one, that is mine."

He turned around to see a small, cute looking monster. She was emerald green, with big, beautiful eyes, and bright pink arms and legs. Out of the top of her head were two pink antennas with love hearts lovingly sat on the top.

"Sorry, I don't mean to be rude, but that is where I sit," the monster said timidly.

"Oh, that's OK. How about I sit next to you?" Daniel offered.

"Yeah, that's not a problem. I'm Slick by the way."

"I'm Daniel. I'm so excited to meet you all."

Slick shook Daniel's hand. The slime dripped off the monster's hand and slowly ran through Daniel's fingers.

"You know, in my world, children would go mad for all this slime. It drives parents crazy." Daniel chuckled as he flung the last of the slime off his hands.

Daniel watched one of the monsters sit down, but the slime dripping from his bottom made him slip off the wooden bench and onto the floor. He showed a thumbs up as a sign that he was OK.

"Damn slime," he muttered to himself. "Why couldn't I have a furry bottom and not a slippery one!" He sat down and everyone seemed to calm.

"We're about to begin," Slick told Daniel.

Daniel sat silently and patiently as he waited to find out what was about to happen.

Everyone was seated and, altogether, they began to say,

"I sometimes can be happy, I sometimes can be sad,

It does not mean I'm good and it doesn't mean I'm bad.

Today I am myself; just me, myself, and I,

No one can tell me I'm not unique, nor tell me not to cry."

Daniel listened carefully as they all said this aloud and thought how wonderfully true it was, in his own life and in the monster life.

Dex stood up with another of his friends; he was bright blue, with yellow spangly arms and legs. He had unique yellow spikes sticking out of the top of his head, each one different. Dex introduced him as Spirit.

Dex and Spirit said hello to everyone and paid attention to Daniel, who they introduced to the group once again. Daniel waved at everyone and shyly lowered his hand.

"We do this once a week," Slick explained. "So, you've come at the right time."

"What do you do?" Daniel asked curiously.

"Well, we all meet at least once a week, just to talk. Sometimes we have things on our minds that we need to talk about. Some of us tell jokes and try to make everyone laugh. Some of us don't like to talk, or come out of our houses, but this gives us a chance to get everyone together and share what is happening in our lives. It means we can share ideas and feelings and help each other," Slick told him. "We call it our Monster Mates Meeting."

"I think it's wonderful," Daniel said happily. "We do something similar at my school. I think it really works."

One after one, a different monster stood up and talked about something that had made them happy or sad that week. It seemed, to Daniel, that this was not just a meeting to discuss why the monsters might feel sad, but also one to celebrate their happiness too. Daniel listened carefully to each of the monsters and what they wanted to tell the group.

Next up, was Charm. He had brilliant blue horns coming out of his head, golden yellow oversized teeth and a long brown body that was met with a tiny pair of denim shorts. He was eager to share his achievement with the group.

"This week," Charm began, in a very well-spoken voice, "I got chosen for the lead role in the school play."

There were cheers, clapping and whooping sounds from around the circle as everyone embraced the achievement of Charm.

"It's about time isn't it, Charm?" said Ruby. "Can I play the leading lady?" The rest of the monsters made kissing sounds. Charm blushed and walked away smiling from horn to horn.

It was nearing the end of every monster having their moment around the circle. There were only a few monsters left. Out of the corner of his eye, Daniel

spotted one of the monsters he hadn't seen before. She looked worried; her hands were trembling, and she seemed to be taking some very deep breaths. He knew exactly how it felt to be worried about something. Daniel wondered what could be worrying her so much in a group of monsters who just seemed to want to help.

Then he realised; the trembling monster was Shelley!

Chapter 5
Shelley Needs Help

Daniel heard Dex call her Shelley, and it seemed to be her turn to talk to the group. Shelley stood up, her trembling could be felt throughout the group.

"Well done, Shelley, for coming today," one of the monsters said. Everyone nodded in agreement and watched as the nervous monster opened her mouth, but nothing came out. She lowered her head and tried again. Everyone held their breath. The trembles started to feel stronger and she began to wring her hands. Daniel worried about Shelley. What could be so wrong that she was this scared to talk in front of her friends? There was no time to ask, as Shelley suddenly bolted.

"Shelley, it's OK! Come back!" Dex shouted after her.

Daniel stood up quickly. He wanted to help. He had seen something like this at school with Scarlett when she was asked to a talk in front of the whole class. Before he knew it, his legs were moving quickly, and he was running after Shelley.

"Wait, Shelley! I want to help!" he panted. Daniel kept running. His heart was beating fast and he was sweating. Daniel knew exactly how Shelley was feeling; he felt it too.

Shelley continued to run until she came to a beautiful, tranquil garden. It was full of nature, calm and peacefulness. It was a breath-taking place.

Daniel caught up. He bent over, with his hands on his knees and tried to catch his breath. He panted but raised his head to take in the beauty around him; this place was magical. Monster Mountain really did have some of the most incredible places. Shelley was sitting on a pristine white bench with her head in her hands, sobbing gently.

"Are you ok, Shelley? Is there anything I can do for you?" asked Daniel gently as he sat beside her.

Shelley lifted her head slowly and looked Daniel straight in the eye. He could see a single tear roll down her face and splash onto her knee.

"It's just, I can't... I can't..." Shelley struggled to find the words. "I don't know how to deal with everyone staring at me. It's too much. My belly feels like jelly all the time, my hands get sweaty and my head hurts."

Daniel thought a moment before he responded. He had felt the same. Maybe if he talked to Shelley about it, she would see that she wasn't alone and that others felt like this too – monsters and humans. Maybe they could help each other.

"You call it jelly, but to me it feels like butterflies fluttering in my belly, but I think it's the same thing, the same feeling," Daniel said with a reassuring smile.

They both smiled at each other and felt a sense of happiness as they realised that they weren't alone with their feelings. They both relaxed around each other; sharing their feelings had helped.

"I get scared too sometimes when I do things, I'm not comfortable with." Daniel continued, "We aren't all the same, so we react differently to situations sometimes. Some people like to be in front of people, but some of us find it difficult. Have you spoken with your friends and told them how you feel?"

"I can't, I feel like a failure," Shelley said sadly.

"You aren't a failure!" Daniel shook his head. "Just the fact you came to the meeting today shows you aren't. I think you need to know that you can do this! Your friends want you to do well, no matter what you say. Nobody will judge you - Dex said before that you should never judge anyone, and he is right. These are your friends; they are supporting you and they want to hear about you."

"I suppose..." Shelley said slowly.

"We all feel things inside our bodies when we do new things or things that make us nervous." Daniel wondered if he was reassuring himself or Shelley. "But some of these feelings are natural. It's our body's way of building excitement in us. If the feelings get too much, which they sometimes do, then we must find ways to control them. Do you know how to control how you feel?"

"It helps to come to this garden. It's calm and it gives me chance to breathe," said Shelley.

"Well, that's a great start!" Daniel said happily. "Why don't we try some deep breaths? I do this to help me get to sleep at night. You must breathe in through your nose and out through your mouth. Try to control your breath as you release it. OK?"

"OK." Shelley nodded.

They sat side by side on the white bench taking deep breaths in through their noses and out through their mouths. They repeated this for a few minutes.

"I think that might be helping. My belly doesn't feel like jelly as much anymore," Shelley said with relief.

"Have you ever done something that makes you really excited?" asked Daniel.

"Yeah, lots of times. I think my favourite was riding on a rollercoaster!" replied Shelley.

"A belly fully of jelly or butterflies can be good feelings too. It can be excitement. Next time you're struggling, and you feel nervous, remember how you felt on the rollercoaster and use that feeling to make your nerves good ones. Ones that make you excited and happy. I think I'm going to try that tomorrow," Daniel confirmed.

"What's tomorrow?" Shelley asked.

"It doesn't matter, let's focus on today!" Daniel said quickly.

"You're very wise." Shelley smiled at him. "You've really helped me, Daniel. Thank you." Daniel felt warm inside, it was good to help.

"Wonderful! I think you should continue to practice this," Daniel said. "It's also important to know that the monsters are your friends; they support you. They don't want you to fail. If you make a mistake, then that is OK too. We are all human, or monsters in your case, but we all make mistakes. Nobody is perfect."

"Thanks, Daniel! Do you mind if I ask you a question?" Shelley asked.

"Of course, you can ask me anything." Daniel nodded.

"How do you know so much about the way I am feeling and how I can deal with it?" Shelley enquired.

"I feel the same way too," Daniel said shyly. He continued, "In fact, I have had this feeling of butterflies in my belly since yesterday. I've tried to ignore it, but it keeps coming back." Just thinking about them made his tummy flutter.

"What's bothering you?" Shelley asked with concern in her eyes.

"I have an assembly tomorrow at school. It's our class assembly and I dread it every year. I must stand in front of the whole school and parents; my heart beats fast, my belly gets butterflies and my hands get sweaty. My mum always tells me that everything will be OK, but sometimes that doesn't help." Daniel rubbed his hands as the feeling of worry crept back.

"You seem so confident though," Shelley stated.

"Well, that is it. Nobody can see what is going on for someone else. These are feelings that aren't always clear to everyone else," Daniel explained.

Daniel realised that this was the first time he had spoken out loud how he felt about the assembly, and was surprised that it made him calmer. He had shared a problem and it had made him feel much better. That he could give Shelley advice about a similar problem made his nerves settle down too. Daniel's friends always told him that he was good at giving advice, but he needed to be able to take his own advice.

"Daniel, I think you need to remember what you told me." Shelley interrupted Daniel's thoughts.

"You sound like my friends!" Daniel smiled.

"It's true. You need to remember your own advice. When you are in assembly, remember everyone watching are people that want to see you happy. They won't judge you," Shelley echoed Daniel's words.

"Thank you, Shelley." Daniel smiled.

"I think you will be wonderful! I have an idea, why don't we both stand together at the campfire and speak in front of everyone? I can talk to the group and you can practice your part for the assembly. We can practice the techniques you told me about and see if they help. We can support each other and get encouragement from the rest of the group." Shelley jumped up off the seat enthusiastically.

"I think that would really help me. Thank you, Shelley," Daniel agreed.

"Let's head back to the campfire," Shelley said.

Just as the two of them were ready to set off to camp, Shelley signalled to Daniel to be still and quiet. Upon the flowers to the right of them, sat a large, stunning butterfly. It seemed magical. Daniel and Shelley gazed in silence at the prettiness that was before them.

"Look at all those colours. It's like a rainbow." Daniel pointed gently with his finger.

"I know!" whispered Shelley. "How many colours can you see?"

"I can see turquoise and purple..." Daniel's voice trailed off.

"There's pink, orange and green there too."

Shelley pointed.

"Look how it shimmers in the light. It's like glitter!" Daniel was amazed.

"It truly is beautiful isn't it?" Shelley confirmed.

Daniel and Shelley walked back towards the camp. They sang the colours of the rainbow song. There was no rush and Daniel wanted Shelley to remain calm. As they walked, Daniel was able to take in the loveliness once again surrounding him. He was fascinated with everything in Monster Mountain. The trees were an array of green and, much to Daniel's pleasure, they didn't look like 'normal' trees. Some were shaped with what looked like upside-down triangles, some had two circular shapes side by side that looked like a pair of glasses, and some stood tall as soldiers with what looked like a hat on the top of them. Daniel smiled to himself. Nothing in Monster Mountain was 'normal', everything was unique. Daniel thought about how, again, this represented the uniqueness of the monsters he had seen and met. It was important to be unique. He needed to accept himself more and just be himself. He was determined to work on this when he returned to his world.

Daniel turned to Shelley and said, "Someone once told me, I think it might be true, that when the rain comes down, the sun appears soon too."

Shelley thought for a moment and said, 'I think that's a lovely way to look at it."

As they grew closer to the campfire, they could hear the rest of the monsters talking amongst themselves. Daniel could feel butterflies in his belly again. He knew Shelley must be feeling the same. He hoped he had done the right thing in agreeing to stand up with Shelley. What if she got upset and ran away again?

Chapter 6
We are in this Together

Shelley and Daniel were nearing the village and could see the campfire burning. The glow of yellow, orange and red was beautiful against the darkness of the night. Daniel felt a tingle from his head to his toes, this village made him feel so much better. He didn't feel scared or worried to be around monsters. He thought about all the times he had assumed monsters were mean and scary. How wrong he had been to have assumed that, just because they were different, he had been afraid. Now, in the moment, he realised he had been wrong to judge. Yes, some of them had more than two eyes, which meant they looked different to what he was used to, but it also meant that they had excellent vision. Daniel chuckled to himself, thinking how useful it would be to have more than two eyes – especially when trying to keep an eye on Darcie! Having more than two eyes must be a great security system; you could literally see anything coming.

"Being different has its advantages, doesn't it?" Daniel said thoughtfully. "I'm just thinking about all the ways you monsters differ to us humans."

"It's so strange that you don't have any slime on you," Shelly told Daniel. "Did you know that having slime helps you do loads of things? Like catch food if it falls or to quickly fix something if it breaks – no need to play hunt-the-glue! And the monsters with loads of fingers? They are the best at maths!"

"I can imagine." Daniel nodded.

"We are like you humans in that we all have our own differences, but we are all caring and kind... and sometimes a bit funny too," Shelley said. "Like how kind everyone was to encourage me to go to the meeting today, they didn't give up on me."

Daniel felt warm inside. It was a wonderful feeling to think of everyone as being totally accepted. He thought about people in his own world; they were the same – kind, funny and caring too.

The other monsters noticed that Daniel and Shelley were on their way back and they began to cheer and wave. Daniel gave a little wave and Shelley offered a shy smile. Daniel thought this was all she could offer at this time because she was probably worrying about standing up in front of everyone. The monsters started to sit back down as Daniel and Shelley entered the circle to take their seats around the campfire.

Daniel cleared his throat, stood up and began to speak. He could see every eye on him as the monsters waited patiently, ready to listen. This was his moment to practice. He took a deep breath, imagined the peace from the gardens filling his body, and began.

"The Tudor period is dated between 1485 and 1603. This was when the Tudors were the ruling family in England. The first Tudor monarch was King Henry VII who claimed the throne when his forces defeated Richard III at the Battle of Bosworth Field in 1485. He ruled until his death in 1509."

The whole campfire was deadly silent as everyone listened to every word that fell from Daniel's mouth.

Once he stopped talking, the monsters clapped and cheered. Daniel could hear shouts of "way to go!" and "well done!" being shouted from round the campfire. He had managed it. He had done what he needed to do, and he felt good. He felt proud and excited.

"That was great!" Dex's voice was louder than the others. "I had no idea what you were talking about, but it sounded very impressive!"

"When Shelley and I spoke," Daniel explained, "she gave me permission to tell you all how she has been feeling. She was upset and worried about standing up in front of us all here today. The feeling she gets when she must talk in front of everyone makes her worried. It's not something that she likes and sometimes it makes her sad, her hands get sweaty and she doesn't think she will be able to do it. That is why she ran away; she was overwhelmed with how she felt, and it all became too much for her. The truth is... I feel like this too when I have to talk to people. Both Shelley and I had a chat in the gardens about ways to deal with feelings of worry and our lack of self-belief. So, Shelley has come back and has decided to overcome her fears and worries and talk to all of us. I think she is very brave."

Daniel stood quietly for a moment to allow the monsters time to think about what he had said. As he waited, a feeling of pride came over him. He had just stood up in front of a group of monsters and had spoken to them. He had remembered his lines perfectly. No fear, no worries, no butterflies. He thought about how he had taken a deep breath before he spoke, how he had thought about the tranquillity of the gardens and how they made him feel at peace. He wasn't afraid. He wasn't alone. He wasn't worrying anymore. The last time he had felt the butterflies was in the garden with Shelley, maybe they had left his belly with the beautiful flowers.

Daniel thought about how if he could do this here, then he could do it with his assembly too. His thoughts were interrupted by the sound of Shelley taking a deep breath and exhaling.

"Come on, Shelley, you can do it!", "we believe in you, Shelley!" and "go for it, Shelley!" could be heard around the campfire as her monster friends all offered their encouragement and support to her.

Shelley stood up, took her place in front of the monsters and began to talk.

"I was going to tell you about my week, but instead I want to say thank you for always supporting me and believing in me. For encouraging me to come to the meeting and always offering your support. Friends can really help you overcome your problems. What Daniel said is true – I do worry about talking in front of you all. I worry I will say something wrong or I will make a mistake or fall over or..."

Shelley tried to continue her long list of worries, but then she heard Ruby say, "I think we all feel like that at times. But we are your friends and we want to listen to you, and we want to help you."

"I know, and that is what Daniel said. I want to thank you for being patient and listening, and to Daniel for helping me overcome some of my worries. I'd like to help him too," Shelley stated.

Daniel smiled at Shelley.

"You've overcome your mountain, Shelley. How lovely is the view!" Daniel whispered into her ear.

Shelley stood for a moment as the realisation of climbing to the top of her mountain hit her. She was overwhelmed with how proud she felt, how the climb up the mountain had been a real struggle, but how incredible the view was from the top. This time, the sense of being overwhelmed was a positive one. She felt amazing to have reached the top of her mountain.

"Daniel has an assembly at school tomorrow, and he is feeling a little nervous. Is there anyone who could offer some ideas of how he could overcome his worries?" Shelley asked the group.

Everyone was stunned by how confident Shelley sounded.

"I think Daniel needs to believe in himself more. He has just spoken in front of all of us and he was amazing!" said Ruby.

"Maybe he could do some deep breaths like he taught you?" suggested Slick.

"How about he thinks of all of us and standing talking to us today?" offered Dex.

Daniel was listening carefully and nodding at the suggestions.

"He should also share his worries with people he cares about," said Charm. "I think that really helps."

Daniel looked around at all the monsters who were willing to offer him help, half of whom he hadn't even met properly yet. He realised that they wanted him to succeed, not fail. They wanted to help and be his friends. Daniel was surprised by the gentle chant that started around the campfire.

"Daniel can do it. Daniel can do it!"

The chant became louder and louder. Daniel jumped up from his seat and shouted, "I CAN DO IT!"

Everyone cheered. Daniel proudly walked back to his seat, next to Shelley, and sat down around the campfire. He had done it and he felt proud. A variety of hands touched his back as they congratulated him on overcoming his fear. Some monsters stood up and high-fived Shelley and Daniel. He turned to Shelley and hugged her, whispering, "thank you," in her ear.

"You helped me too," she replied.

“How do you feel now?” asked Daniel.

“Like I can overcome anything with my friends by my side. How about you?” she questioned.

“Well, I think the butterflies have finally flown away from my belly,” Daniel said with a smile.

“That’s good. How do you feel about the assembly tomorrow?” Shelley asked.

“I think I can do it. I will be nervous, but I think they will be good nerves,” Daniel said with confidence.

“Someone once told me, I think it might be true, that when the rain comes down, the sun appears soon too.” Shelley smiled at Daniel, acknowledging what he had said to her earlier on their way back from the garden.

The atmosphere around the campfire was lively and happy. The monsters began to return to their seats. Dex had caught their attention and everyone settled down to listen. Daniel felt happy, he knew he had friends here. He wasn’t alone anymore, and he wasn’t afraid. Daniel knew that no matter what the problem, they were all in this together.

He wriggled in his seat to get comfy, looked up at Dex and smiled.

Chapter 7
Just Breathe

Dex stood up and gave a thumbs up to Daniel.

"So, I think it is really wonderful that Shelley and Daniel were able to overcome their fears and share their feelings. Lots of us can sometimes feel nervous or worried. How about we all share how we feel after we've told someone about our worries? Anyone want to start?" Dex questioned.

Hands flew up in the air and slime from some of the monsters flung around the campfire. Some of the monsters licked it off their bodies whilst others looked disgusted at it. Daniel smiled as he wiped a dollop of red slime from his rosy red cheeks. He had never had slime slung about in class when his classmates put their hands up, so this was quite different.

"When I tell people how I feel, it makes whatever was on my mind feel less daunting," exclaimed Charm.

"I like it when I confess about a worry and people offer suggestions I hadn't thought about," Dex added.

"Sometimes just saying it helps me to see it from a different angle," Ruby said. "And makes me feel less alone."

"It's great that sharing our feelings can make us all feel so much better," Dex said. "How about we all give Daniel some quick tips for his assembly tomorrow?"

"I would suggest focusing on one thing in the

and take a breath." Then he started to whisper,

"Before you go, you must know,
We're here for you, wherever you go.
Say goodbye until we meet,
Your help tonight is now complete.
Take a breath and close your eyes,
Make a wish and you will fly.
Back to your bed you will go,
Safe and warm in the night-time glow."

Daniel closed his eyes; the darkness took him.

Daniel awoke, he sat up and looked around. He was back in his own bed, in his own room and in his own house. He was already excited to tell Darcie about his dream. Daniel climbed out of bed, already anticipating what might happen in his dreams tonight, and he couldn't help but smile. For now, he needed to get ready for school and tackle his very own mountain; the school assembly.

Chapter 8
Daniel's Mountain

Daniel rushed into the bathroom to get himself ready for school. He looked at himself in the mirror, said, 'You can do this, Daniel', wiped his face and eagerly walked out of the bathroom.

"Daniel! Darcie! Breakfast!" Mum shouted up the stairs.

Daniel bounced down each step, eager to get the day started. Darcie followed shortly after, moaning about something to do with her teddy bears not giving her enough room in bed last night. Darcie always woke up looking like she had been through a bush; her hair stuck up, she had dribble marks on her face and she looked grumpy. Daniel often wondered what adventures she must go on in her dreams to look like that in the morning. He hoped one night she would visit a hairdresser on her adventures. This was just the way she looked every morning and Daniel knew that she wasn't a morning person. He was lucky to get a grunt out of her in the morning.

"Morning, you two," Mum said.

"Morning, Mum," replied Daniel.

"Morning, Mummy," Darcie grumbled.

"We all set for school this morning?" Dad asked as he sipped his tea.

"I sure am!" Darcie nodded.

SCHOOL

"Me too," said Daniel.

Mum seemed surprised at how excited and lively Daniel was feeling about the assembly. It wasn't like him, but she was pleased to see he was embracing that butterflies can sometimes be good feelings too.

They sat as a family of four eating their breakfast, drinking their morning drink and talking about their days ahead. Daniel recalled the family meal last night and how differently he had felt then. He had been anxious and afraid, too worried to even eat. He looked at each of his family members and thought about how 'normal' they were compared to his monster friends in his dream last night. He missed their uniqueness and, just as he was about to tell Darcie about them, Mum interrupted his thoughts.

"Are you ready for the assembly today, Daniel?"

"Yeah, I still feel a little nervous but I'm just going to take a few deep breaths and try my best," Daniel said.

"That's a great attitude, son." Dad sounded proud.

"We can't wait to see you!" Mum said.

Butterflies began to flutter in Daniel's tummy, these were excited butterflies. He had never been excited about an assembly before!

"Let's go! Everyone in the car!" Mum shouted.

Darcie and Daniel arrived at the school playground, happy and eager to see their friends. They liked school; Daniel more than Darcie. As soon as they reached the gates, they ran off to their friends who were shouting their names.

Mum called after them, "See you in there, Daniel! Darcie, be good for Mrs Postlethwaite!"

A loud ringing sound echoed across the playground as each child filed into their class lines like soldiers being called to attention. Daniel looked back at his mum, for one last moment of reassurance, she put her thumb up and smiled. Daniel gave a shy smile and walked into class.

"Right everyone, remember your places and do your best," Mr Grisly, their teacher, directed.

Daniel and the rest of his class were the first in the hall. This was always the way when it was someone's assembly. The hall seemed bigger. Daniel looked around and felt a flutter in his stomach. He took a moment to himself to remember what he had learnt from the monsters. He knew the butterflies were coming back, but he also knew how to control them now. He took some deep breaths, thought about what he wanted to say and remembered he could only try his best. He knew that butterflies were nice feelings too and he thought back to how good he felt last night talking in front of the monsters.

Luke leant over and whispered, "I'm a little nervous."

"Me too," said Daniel.

"Me three," echoed Joe.

"Nerves can be a good thing too though," Daniel whispered to his friends.

This made Daniel realise that he wasn't alone in what he was feeling, just as the monsters had said last night. He leant over to his friends and said, "Take a deep breath and do your best." They smiled at each other and faced forward. He looked around the hall at the colours on the wall. He said each colour to himself in his head, just as he and Shelley had done the night before with the butterfly. Looking for different colours, and repeating them to himself as he waited, made him calm and happy. He hummed the colours of the rainbow song to himself.

Parents filled the hall and there were echoes of conversations bouncing off the walls as parents settled into their seats. There were screams and cries as younger children waited impatiently for the assembly to start. Daniel could see parents trying to quieten down the younger children, usually with something to eat. The rest of the school started to pile in and sit in long rows, according to their classes. Daniel spotted Darcie in the crowd and she beamed with pride. Her smile reached from ear to ear as she was about to watch her big brother have his moment. The crowd settled down and a deafening silence fell as the headteacher walked into the hall. This was it; this was Daniel's moment to climb his mountain.

"Good morning everyone and welcome to the assembly of the Sycamore Class."

Daniel's class began their assembly which was about the Tudors. Daniel listened intently as the other members of his class took their turns. He noticed some had trembling hands, others spoke with confidence and some stumbled over their words. Everyone in the audience smiled. Daniel continued to take some deep breaths, focused on his parents in the crowd and stood up to say his part.

"The Tudor period is dated between 1485 and 1603. This was when the Tudors were the ruling family in England. The first Tudor monarch was King Henry VII who claimed the throne when his forces defeated Richard III at the Battle of Bosworth Field in 1485. He ruled until his death in 1509."

Daniel was clear and calm as he spoke. He returned to his seat feeling a sense of overwhelming pride that he had managed to say his part and enjoyed doing it. He thought back to how he had taken deep breaths and focused on his parents; the exact advice the monsters

had offered him and Shelley the previous evening. The assembly continued, but Daniel was lost in thought! His mind wandered to Dex, Shelley, Ruby and all the others. He couldn't wait to return to see them; he was desperate to tell them all about his assembly and how he used their advice to help him get over his very own mountain. He hoped he would get to visit them again that evening and share his success with them.

From the top of his mountain, he could see endless happy faces and it felt amazing! People were proud of him and this was the best view he could possibly have seen; their happiness and his own.

The end

Acknowledgement

Writing a book that is so close to my heart, personally, makes it even more poignant. I hope those that read this book realise they are not alone, that there is hope and that one day the rain will stop, and the sun will come out.

To Erin, my beautiful daughter, my life, my love, and my greatest achievement. You bring such fun, laughter, and love into my life. Never stop being your sweet, kind, caring, funny and sassy self. I love you endlessly.

To Steve, my amazing partner, the one who pushes me to seek happiness in my dreams. Without your love, unwavering support, and dedication, I wouldn't have got to this point. I love you for all that you do and all that you are to me.

To my Mum and Dad, who are the foundation of our family, who offer love, wisdom, and a family unit I am incredibly proud to be part of. I am thankful for every time you have encouraged me, pushed me to achieve my goals and supported me in life.

To my siblings and their partners, thank you for all your support, love, and guidance. For all the times you've wiped away tears, made me laugh, given me memories and pushed me to aim for the stars. To Ebony, Freddie, Alfie, and Isaac, thank you for the endless laughs, craziness and love you bring to my life. To Tanya, for always being you; the most loyal and wonderful best friend any girl could ask for.

To Aaliyah, Liam, and Jayden, I love you.

Thanks to everyone on the Bear with Us team who helped, guided, and supported me so much. Special thanks to Andy, the ever-patient project manager and fastest email replier ever. To Lor, my amazing editor, who guided me throughout the project with kindness and support. Yogesh, who created illustrations and characters into something I had only ever imagined it to be. To Richie, Christian and Gillian for working your magic.

Finally, to my readers, thank you for your unwavering support. I hope you enjoy the book.

Child Acknowledgement List

To all the wonderful children out there who are now a part of my book; thank you. Embrace your individuality and uniqueness, and always be you!

Erin Frankish
Milo McDonald
Martha McDonald
Rosie Lowdnes
Isaac Ashworth
Riley Halpin
Jem Winstanley
Cora Winstanley
Aria Winstanley
Albie Winstanley
Leon Mullen
Jacob Khwaja
Angel Shaw
Kal-el Shaw
Oliver Stephens
Corben Jones
Jayden McCormick
Xander Barlow
Louis Barlow
Olsen Faulkner
Orla Faulkner
Keira Murphy
Poppy Roe
Thomas Roe
Ciaran Adams
Saoirse Adams
Amelia Moffat
Matilda McLellan
Caila McLellan
Jess Tweed
Kirtys Barnett
Corbyn Barnett
Louis Kirk
Alice Kirk
Sadie Kirk
Orla Palmer
Chloe Jones-Williams
Felix Alexander
Williams-Jenkins
Willow Mondryk
Penny Mondryk
Elijah Allen
Ophelia Allen
Miller Shaw-Murfitt
Tilda Shaw-Murfitt
James Lawrenson

Phoebe Forrest
Alfie Forrest
James Winstanley
Joshua Winstanley
Joel Winstanley
Jack Winstanley
Sophia Mann
Alexia Mann
Freddie Mann
Toby Forrester
Tyler Gray
Amber Loughman
Harper Walsh
Freya Tobin
Alix Leung
Elaina Leung
Eden Taylor
Mason Peacock
Rio Noble
Bobby Noble
Nora Floodgate
Harry Southworth-Mills
Amelia Southworth-Mills
Blossom O'Shaughnessy
Scarlett Potter
Amelia Potter
Alana Jay Taggart
Mylah Stella Keenan
Millie Dee Keenan
Emelia Hulston- Kenyon
Phoenix Barratt
Poppy Barratt
Charlie Kirk
Rylee Kirk
Ethan Stock- Collins
Charlie Collins
Lincoln Lewis
Esmae George

Kyran Wegener
Talia Wegener
Bobby Tinsley
Alfie Tinsley
Arabella Wegener
Oliver Stone
Freddie Stone

Poppy Rawson
Olli Rawson
Luna Johnson
Parker Brotherton
Orion Young
Skylar Young
Riley Moffat-Mullertz
Kya Moffat-Mullertz
Cooper Hopkins
Leah Claypole
Lara Claypole
Halle Claypole
Chloe White
Isabelle Willerton
Harriet Willerton
Freya Hindle
Harrison Hindle
Primrose Schaffner
Madison Plachotny
Ollie Plachotny
Jasper Caimin Sierotko-Cadd
Jessie Tweed
Edith Shember
Mathilda Shember
Joseph Hunter
Matthew Hunter
Bobby Gradwell
Ivy Gradwell
Charlotte North
Olivia North
Leighton North
Paige Sierotko
Axel Behan
Maya Roper
Ayden Roper
Ethan Longworth
Alice Williams
Isla Williams

Belle Forrest
Dougie Forrest
Jackson Smith
Serina Dobson
Natalie Dobson
Harry Thomas
Emelia Thomas

Adam Lawrenson
Ria Stonehouse
Molly Gallagher
Thomas Gallagher
Mia-Jay Hurst
Violet Hurst
Lewis George Buckley
Lyla Scanlan
Rosie Quinn
Daisy Quinn
Ebony Jones
Freddie Jones
Alfie Brown
Evie Meakin
Miller Meakin
Noah Oldfield
Louie Oldfield
Daniel Smith
Hollie Smith
Isla-Mae Johnson
Emmie Snape
Niamh Snape
Zach Snape
Isla-Grace Robinson
Joshua Staniforth
Jasmyn Hilton
Hendrix Hilton
Poppy McDermott
Jaxx McDermott
Roman McDermott
Caitlin Jones
Amelia Jones
Macy Lloyd
Phoebe Lloyd
Poppy Lloyd
Joseph Lloyd
Quinn Rhodes
Grace Gavin
Poppy Gavin
Callum Walker
Charlie Walker
Khadija Faheem Aslam
Asiya Faheem Aslam
Bailey Cornthwaite
Freddie Cornthwaite
Izzy Cornthwaite
Ella Cornthwaite
Charlotte Wallis
Isabelle Wallis
Tadhg Loftus
Freddie Loftus
Vincent Isaac Ennis
Jack Stone
Joshua Stone
Jake Scott-Jones
Mia Scott-Jones
Archie Walkden
Ivy-Grace Walkden
Brooke Lowndes
Caleb Malaney
Emeyliah Flynn
Brayden Alexander
Jet Pham
Leon Pham
Aysia Willis
Annie O'Brien
Alfie Newton
Frankie Scott
Lilly Ellison
Ivieh Mary Ellor
Jaxson Higgins
Mary-Jayne McCabe
Arthur Hardy
Heidi Roberts
Ben Henrick
Ted Henrick
Freya Rose Davison
William Edwards
Connor McDonald
Lexi-Marie Shaw
Luca Whittaker
Pippa Whittaker
Logan Devane
Victoria Liane Warburton
Logan Yates
Oscar Jacques
Ellis Shaw
Isla Hazel Booth
Keira Bretherton
Ayden Bretherton
Tilly Bretherton
Dakota Charles
George O'Brien
Oliver Penny
Zoe Fossati
Jaxon Fossati
Asa Saxton
Isaac Saxton
Zaviae Jamieson
Carter Challoner
Kadi-Leigh O'Gara
Ada Latham
Grace Crossley
Parkey Rex Gilligan
Joshua Parker
Reece Dodds
Emily Dodds
Remy Aldridge
Callan Aldridge
Lily Tongue
Rose Tongue
Lucas Tongue
Eleanor Bantoft
Zachary Leevy-Oliver
Bobby Hyde
Francesca Hyde
Megan Lawley
Sophie Lawley
Ethan Stocks-Collins
Shay Briggs
Lexi Briggs
Codie Briggs
Martha Swallow
Henry Jones-McGrory
Evie Jones
George Jones
Thea O'Brien
Cobyjohn Hanvey
Logan Harrison
Roman Inglis
Grace Julia Ainsworth
Louie David Ainsworth
Scarlett Jade Riley
Tyler France
Madison Gribben
Scarlett Stacey-Brown
Aadhi Vekaria
Aanya Vekaria
Owen Bridgeman
Chloe Bridgeman
Coby Tindall
Joshua Tindall
Ellie-Rose Raftery
Jason Souter
Zoe Cristina Domingos
Phoebe Byrne
Parker Byrne
Isla- Grace Roscoe
Marnie Ava Roscoe
James Loughman
Izzie Taylor
Vincent Roy Skolosdra
George Bratt
Marnie Beech
Freddie Parker
Toby Goggins

Vanessa India Ennis
Arthur Moss
Christian Sykes
Jasmine Morris
Alice Duffy
Maisie Foy
Liliana Foy
Holly Marie King
Evelyn Cowdell-Murray
Taylor Jennings
Shannan Rennie
Bethan Rennie
Rihannan Rennie
Coban Rennie
Teegan Rennie
Kaitlan Rennie
Noah Hangle
Theo Hangle
Archie Howarth
Amelia Howarth
Alan Howarth
Imogen Andrews
Jonty Andrews
Ezra Bowen-Sadler

James Oxley
Lucy Oxley
Ella Grace Kennedy
Zeke Anthony Kennedy
Mason Rodney Wilson
Isabelle Ahern
Mylo Ahern
Jack Marshall
Charlie Marshall
Oscar Marshall
Samuel Moss
Emilia Moss
Ariella Marchbank
Elijah Marchbank
Dominic Madden
Caleb Nicholson
Jonas Nicholson
Pranav Rana
Pranaya Rana
Delilah Crawford
Franklin Crawford
Ozzy Harrison
Axl Harrison
Reggie Barsted
Sophia Happer
Maisie Happer
Hannah Fry
Olivia Fry

Purdey Fleur Gilligan
Rory Steven Whittaker
Zander Daniel Whittaker
Bailey Kay
Lilly Hawley
Lexi Garside
Harrison Dott
Jacob Dott
Noah Davenport
Lennon Swallow
Riley Mapletoft
Sophia Davis
Amelia Orange
Archie Orange
Daniel Hand
Emily Hand
Scarlett Simpson
Daniel Simpson
Daniel Evans
Megan Evans
James McNulty
Skye Kershaw
Logan West
Finley West

Xander Nevett-Brown
Monty Nevett-Chapman
Nathaniel Bradbury-Adams
Brodie Howie
Jemma Howie
Matthew (Busta) Howie
Jaxson Howie
Aden Howie
Oliver Howie
Amelia Howie
Freddie Rushton
Henry Rushton
Bertie Trenell
Constance Trenell
Amelie Hampson
Sofia Hampson
Lucia Ambrosino
Chiara Ambrosino
Jacob Mollart
Jasmine Mollart
Catherine Mollart
Grace Clarke
Tilly Clarke
Ralph McCubbin
Darcy McCubbin
Freddie James Clowes
Emilia Gorski
Adam Gorski

Lisa Goggins
Maisie Leigh Roberts
Oscar Joe Roberts
Ralphie Joe Roberts
Finley Donovan
Keira Donovan
Shayne Chandler-Curley
Noah Chandler-Curley
Kaitlin Hatton
Troy Hatton
Summer Martin
Adam Joseph Newton
Tomas James Newton
Ashton Robert Newton
Alisha Sargent
Mikeala Sargent
Jacob Sargent
Lucio Liguori
Mia Bell
Oscar Wright
Jenson Wright
Mia Lyon
Cruze Hansen
Chayce Charles William Purnell
Maisy Kelly
Isabelle Kelly
Freddie Kelly
Thomas Towns
Robbie Wilson
Leo Wilson
Elijah Wilding
Ollie Rhodes-Bennett
Harlee-Elizabeth Thorpe
Lilly Boulton
Kayden Boulton
Brogan Boulton
Sebastian Raybould
Teddy Grey
Harrison Baker
Jacob Baker
Eleanor Stallman
Olivia Stallman
Hunter Hanaghan
Marnie-Lee Garside
Jameson Garside
Sofia Puckeridge
Levi Puckeridge
Sophia Wilkinson
Marcella Wilkinson
Harvey Chapman
Daisy Chapman
Patsy Brough

Phoebe Basnett
Charlotte Basnett
Torvi Mable
Remus Williams
Kyden Edwards
James Blockley
Emilie Blockley
Maya Skinner
Oliver Bolshaw
Max Josef
Skye Tompkins
Aoife Kenny
Tadhg Kenny
Jack Tipton
Lily-Mae Tipton
Imogen Shuttleworth
Hattie Shuttleworth
Florence Wallace
Isla Wallace
Florence Coghlan
Bertie Coghlan
Sebastian Muldoon
Benjamin Muldoon
Samuel Muldoon
Athena Gardiner-Shepherd
Cian-James MacDonald
Freya Regan
Angus Regan
Declan Regan
Hunter John Thorley
Elise Jade Thorley
Grace Booth
Lucy Booth
Louis Crowther
Archie Crowther
Thomas England
Matylda Stables
Kallani Barlow
Kyra-Paige Barlow
Brady-Lee Barlow
Corby Barlow
Toby McLoughlin
Poppy McLoughlin
Malachi Malata
Jeremiah Malata
Jacob Harry Flood
Maizy Fitzgerald
Oscar Worth
Ollie Worth
Quincy Taylor
Eleanor Wadsworth
Marcus Williams
Anya Williams

Brooke Walker
Blake Houghton
Tilly Piff
Xavier Hensman
Marcus Gough
Henry Gough
Merrick Graham
Neisha Graham
Leila Windsor
Sydney Windsor
Jack Mouten
Benjamin Faulkner
Arlo Faulkner
Ezra Faulkner
Lucy Davies
Ella Davies
Hetty Burdock
Bronte Burdock
Phoebe Burdock
Summer Fenton
Macey Fenton
Cody Fenton
Imogen Gough
Macie Bolton
Harry Fletcher
Lottie Fletcher
Rhys Jones
Thea Jones
Lyra Jones
Jacob Turner
Georger Turner
James Wood
George Wood
Harrison Bromiley
Mia-Sarah Bromiley
Amela Cardon
Jasper Cardon
Zuha Rafiq
Zaynab Rafiq
Harper Harrison
Elara-Rose Harrison
Charlie Heath
Harper Heath
Archie Heath
Oliver Grant
Lucas Grant
Hunter Hanaghan
Alice Scott
Eli Barnes
Ewan Barnes
Brady Brocklehurst
Leo Brocklehurst
Elliot Robins

Evangelene Brough
Oscar Brough
Billy Blaikie
Manny Moore
Arun Odedra
Sami Odedra
Joshua Lewis
Lincoln Jack Lewis
Lilly May Lewis
Teddy Beko
Roo Beko
Vic Beko
Harry Bramwell
Evelyn Bramwell
Tommy Reed
Henry Sheratt
Levi Roberts
Kyson Roberts
Sienna Bullivent
Ethan Bullivent
Joshua Johnson
Arla Watson
Enya Watson
Ralph Mottershead
Eliza Mottershead
Grace Slater
George Hughes
Leo Marsh
Abigail Marsh
George Wright
Rosie Wright
Max Woods
Harry Woods
Freddie Woods
Lilly Woods
Rory Machin
Luke Machin
Evie Rossetti-Anderson
Rocco Rossetti-Anderson
James Alexander
Toby Alexander
Ewan Holmes
Finnley Holmes
Harper Holmes
Olivia O'Sullivan
Daniel O'Sullivan
Ada Cunningham
Leland Heuerman-Gratton
Lottie Neal
Zachary Wood
Elliott Wood
Brodie Holland
Charlie Emerson

Eva-Lee Sharp
Milly Wadsworth
William Wadsworth
Ralph Mottershead
Eliza Mottershead
Penelope Brookes-Wilde
Charlie Andrew
Anthony Brewer
Preston Paul William Mellor
Ivy-Rose Barbra Mellor
Roman Mellor
Tai Mellor
Piper Mellor
Faith Williams
Dougie Williams
Amelia Nicklin
Ava Nicklin
Riley Simpson
Theodore Simpson
Keeley Tonge
Leela Tonge
Finley Twigg
Sebastian Twigg
Keeva Parker
Kinsey Parker
Alyssa Gledhill
Alfie Gledhill
Oliver Lee
Sam Lee
Shane Koo
Ezra Ali-Hookens
Billy Love
Claire Gould
Lillian Gould
Tamia-Leah Alexander
Taye Alexander
Holly Ritchie
Alex Ritchie
Rosco Thornhill
Bailey Thornhill
Florence Broadhead
Nell Broadhead
Coen Fenwick
Amber Greenhalgh
Owen GreenHalgh
Summer Concannon
Alistair Flaherty
Mason Jackson
Logan Jackson
Isabelle Challis
Freddie Challis
Amelia Whittaker
Emily Connolly

Flynn Robins
Lucas Robins
Kaia Robins
Winston Simcock
Alexis Simcock
Charlie Walton
Ruby Wain

Wilfred Wain
Immie Wymbs
Annabelle Wymbs
Lawrence Thomas Litherland
Bradley Hughes
Paige Hughes
Izzabella Watt
Daizy-Lou Watt
Freddy Watt
Elisza-Blu Watt
Poppy-Lee Brown
Harry Woodward
Harper Woodward
Olly Davies
Archie Eadie
Mia Jackson
Taylor Jackson
Eliza Millen
Freya Millen
Alfie Oldfield
Ollie Fritz
Faith Passi
Amadea Passi
Levi Passi
Malak Elgammal
Myar Elgammal
Amelia Tabois
Jessica Tabois
Samuel Tabois
Felix Booini
Max Booini
Jesse Fox
Alanna White
Brian White
Isabella White
Ayesha Khurshid
Aqeel Khurshid
Ammara Khurshid
Alexia Thorpe
Sasha Thorpe
Ella Noaln
Sophie Nolan
Jessica Nolan
Oliver Roberts
Lorena Roberts

Shanahan Medloby
Sienna Crowe
Leona Crowe
Bethany Shields
Lucas Shields
Arthur Galleymore
Isla Galleymore

Georgia May Obbard
Gracie Leigh Obbard
Roman Donnelly
Phoebe Hume
Toby Hume
Vincent Randall
Marley Jones
Willow Jones
Poppy Susans
Riley Walter
Cody Walter
Jack Taylor
Olivia Taylor
Abbi Walker
Kaci Walker
Bobby Krupa
Lexia Benson
Elsie May Harrison
Huey Shaw
Ronnie Shaw
Ronnie Sebes
Penny Chui
Leo Chui
Dieter Flower
Simone Flower
Ilaria Messina
Neave Smith
Xavier Kairouz
William Harry Andrew
Natalia- Maria Skourti
Liam Naulty
Amelia Naulty
Isabella Warwick
Sophie Warwick
Kiara-Grace Plummer
Tyler Cole
Tate Cole
Max Cain
Amelia-Rose Lowndes
Isla-Mae Lowndes
Olivia May Pearson
Ryan Vine
Cameron Vine
Kobie Johnson
Eliza Zaman

Isabella Niamh Patricia Byrne
Erica Fox
Niamh Moriarty
Madison Hulland
Kendall Hulland
Sienna Louise Roles
Noah James Collett
Amelie Sharp
Lewis Sharp
Freyah Bradley
William Graham
Beatrix Graham
Jude Lawrence
Ottilie Rose Lawrence
Mitchell Finney
Max Hulme
Sofia Anwar
Charlie Coleman
Lily Coleman
Freddie Sadler-Kean
Minnie Sadler-Kean
Elliot Sadler-Kean
Mia Marie Self
Phoebe Rose Self
William Self
James Corbelt
Laila Kamara
Haris Kamara
Koby O'Connell
Heidi Quinn
Chaylea Senior
Tiana-Jay Senior
Delylah Stones
Zakariah Ali-Hayes
Stanley Tidman
Alina Tidman
Leia Addison
Lila Kaine-Morrlly
Ryli Kaine-Morrlly
Bodi Kaine-Morrlly
Aria Buckley
Charlie Ingham
Keira Ingham
Riley Bridges
Carter Martin
Jesse Davies
Isabella Davies
William Davies
Marcelo Reffell
Ricardo Reffell
Oscar Linard
Aela Lelievre
Mason Jay Gregory-Tatton

Logan Rogers
Riley Rogers
Jack Heaney
Harriet Heaney
Joseph Heaney
Thomas Heaney
William Heaney
Teddy Heaney
Francis Heaney
Gracie Heaney
Carys Best
Seren Best
Oliver Taylor
Freddie Davidson
George Davidson
Theo Davidson
Nevaeh Wellington
Taio Wellington
Noah Carrey
Grayson Carrey
Amber Hayes
Carys Trafford-Pritchard
Katie Trafford-Pritchard
Holly Trafford-Pritchard
John Ainsworth
James Ainsworth
Poppy Grinsted
Heidi Grinsted
Freddie Grinsted
Albie Grinsted
Hanna Humphreys
Hattie Humphreys
Gianluca Altobelli
Gisele Altobelli
Oliver Thompson
Ella Thompson
Evie Thompson
Alex Young
Iris Young
Hallie Jayne Mitchell Phillips
Poppy Roberts
Aidan Paddison
Ewan Paddison
Thomas Howells
Freddie Howells
Isa Farah
Jack Brooklyn Hoskins
Sienna Roach
Hadley Roach
Aiden Smith
Amelia Smith
Devishi Bhalotia
Robbie Semple

Emilene Zaman
Charlotte Collins
Benjamin Collins
Oliver Flynn Carter
Sophia Rae Carter
Jasmine Pickles
Robin Pickles
Jack Ian George
Haydn Carter Jones
Phoenix Pownall
Keswick Pownall
Miley-Rose Jenkinson
Jonah Jenkinson
Ezra Jenkinson
Dylan Gibson-George
Barry Lynch
Laura Lynch
Sonny Butterworth
Joshua Scannell
Ruby Scannell
Joshua Rust
Elliot Rust
Harvey Wilson-Brown
Orly Thompson
Blake Hyland
Eli-James Hyland
Noah Carrington
Elise Carrington
Ivy Carrington
Tyler-James Burney
Jasmine Burney
Chloe Hayward
Jamie Hayward
Isabelle Hayward
Jack Griffiths
Alexander Colegate
James O'Flynn
Michael-Jon Hayes
Mayleen Blankley
Noah Blankley
Emily Forrester
Edward Forrester
Mason Jay Tatton
Aurora Raine Ciampoli
Rio Xavier Heinrich Henry
Eva Parente e Coelho
Henrique Parente e Coelho
Luke O'Reilly
Enzo Ellis
Troy Murphy
Olli Calvert
Willow Calvert
Autumn Calvert

Evelyn Cowton
Elijah Buggy
Arcadia Passier
Linnea Brooke Carriere

Logan X Baxter
Sydney Melanson
Ryan Melanson
Mischa D'Rozario
Minnie D'Rozario
Lila Dornan-O'Neill
Rose Dornan-O'Neill
Harry Fellowes
Isabel Fellowes
Shakir Moledina
Alayna Moledina

Tayne Tuki
Jayde Tuki
Fiadh Preedy
Sullivan Cyril
Chichester-Knight
Kaitlyn Giles
Ciaran Wilcox
Aodhan Wilcox
Alexander Lykouras
Nanda Lykouras
Charlotte Hall
Cameron Hall
Patience Shaw
Andrew Shaw
Amaanah Visram
Nemah Visram

Mia Gibney-Brown
Chloe Armstrong
Mia Nicolls
Joey Nicolls

Maisy Mulholland
Connie Mulholland
Jaxon Barlow
Charlie Daniel
Freddie Harry
Adam Hunter
Maisie Gavranich
Conor Hand
Rory Hand
Rehmah Visram

To all the ladies and gentlemen who trusted me with their child's name,
who wanted to support me and believed in my book; thank you.
I hope you enjoy reading this book as much as I enjoyed writing it.

Much Love
Leanne Brown